Use these stickers for the activities in the book

Page 2

Page 3

ss

s ss

Page 5

Page 7

br

dr dr

Page 8

th th

th th

Page 19

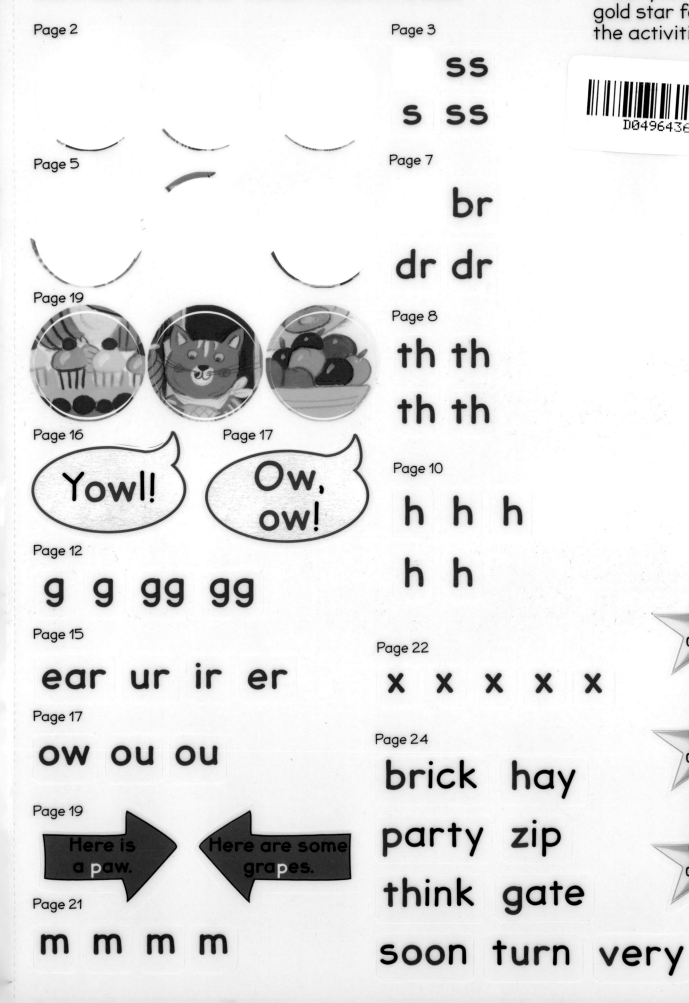

Page 16

Yowl!

Page 17

Ow, ow!

Page 10

h h h

h h

Page 12

g g gg gg

Page 15

Page 22

ear ur ir er

x x x x x

Page 17

Page 24

ow ou ou

brick hay

Page 19

Here is a paw.

Here are some grapes.

party zip

think gate

Page 21

m m m m

soon turn very

Well done!

Well done!

Well done!

Get Set Go Phonics

Puss in Boots

Phonics Consultant: Susan Purcell

Illustrator: Kay Widdowson

Concept: Fran Bromage

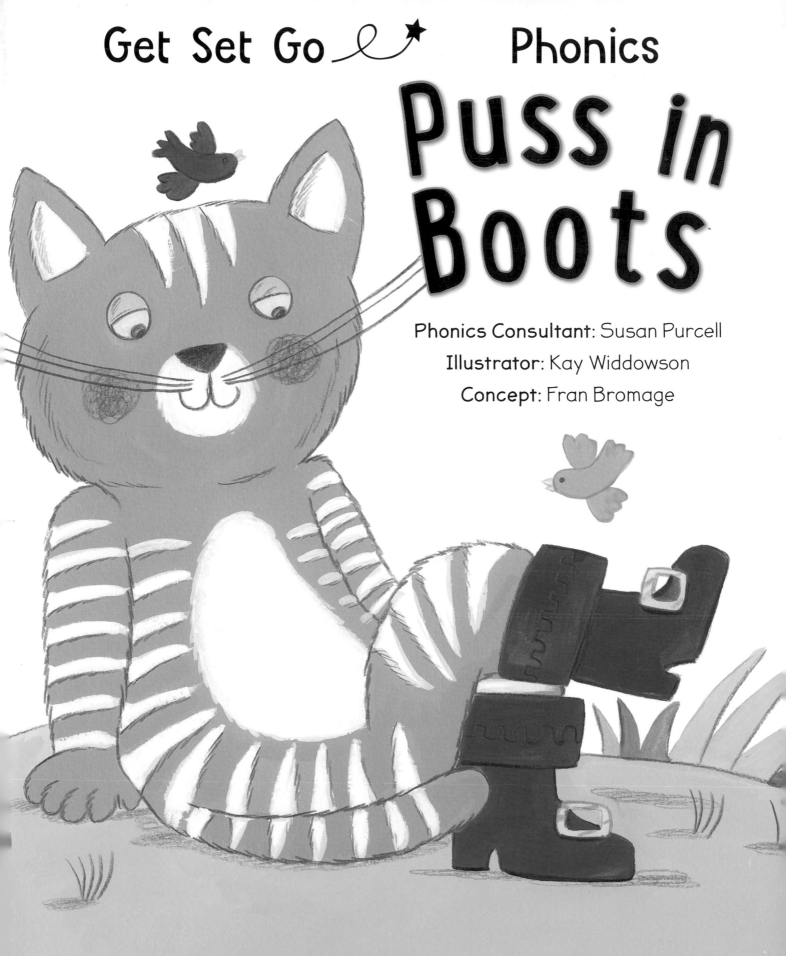

Miles Kelly

Once upon a time, there was a miller who had three sons called Simon, Sid and Sam. When the miller died, he left the mill to Simon and his donkey to Sid.

Say the names as you spot each son.

Stick on their stickers.

2

Simon

Sid

Sam

Sam was left with the miller's cat, Puss. "Silly old cat, what use are you?" said Sam.

Imagine Sam's surprise when Puss replied, "Pass me a sack and get me some boots and you will soon see!"

What a good try! Put a gold star here.

Use the stickers to **spell** some words beginning or ending in s.

 **s**and    **s**ock   class   dre**ss**

3

So Sam gave his cat a big sack and some red boots.

Puss put carrots in the sack and set off to catch a rabbit.

Sound out these words, which all use the k sound made by c and k.

car   coat   castle

keep   kick   jacket   luck

Puss went to the castle with his catch and presented it to the king, as a gift from the Marquis of Carabas. The king was delighted.

Well done!

cat

buckle

king

5

The next day, Puss brought Sam to the river. Puss knew the king and princess would drive past soon.

"But I can't swim very well!" said Sam bravely, as Puss dragged him into the water.

Say the names of the things in the picture, as you spot them.

brick   **bridge**   **dragonfly**
dress   **driver**

"I might **drown**!" shouted Sam. Puss **dropped** Sam's clothes behind a **bramble** bush, just as the king's coach **drove** over the **bridge**.

done!

Use your stickers to **spell** some words beginning with **br** and **dr**.

brush   **br**other   **dr**um   **dr**ip

Try to hear the soft th sound (as in think)

Thank you for stopping!

Puss blocked the path of the king's coach.

"Thieves have pushed the Marquis of Carabas into the river," he shouted. "I think he's drowning!"

Sound out the words thin and they. Can you hear the difference?

Use the stickers to **spell** some words with the soft th sound.

 thin   thick    thorn   third

 8

The king's servants threw Sam a rope and pulled him onto the bank. They fetched him clean clothes too.

Listen for the oo sound (as in boot)

Sam looked like a true Marquis in his blue boots. Then, the king asked him into the coach.

Well done!

Sound out these words, which all use the oo sound.

glue   clue   flew   chew

soon   room   hoop

9

Draw attention to the h sound (as in happy)

Puss was happy his plan was working. He went up the hill and spoke to the workers gathering hay.

Use the stickers to **spell** some words beginning with the h sound.

hug   hop   hen   hat   hit

Whose land is this?

"Please say this is the Marquis of Carabas' land," whispered Puss to the workers, so they did.

The king was dazzled by this news.

Well done!

Sound out these words containing the z sound.

zip   zoo   fizz   buzz
zigzag   these   cheese

11

Puss ran off again – this time to a castle where he knew a big ogre lived. Puss knocked loudly at the gate and a servant let him in.

Use the stickers to **spell** some words with the g sound.

goose   give   buggy   egg

Puss was shown into the ogre's room and climbed up onto the oak table.

"So, what is it you need to know?" asked the ogre.

Please show me some magic!

Sound out these words with the oa sound.

go   no   toe   note

goat   boat   grow   blow

Puss said, "I've heard you can turn yourself into anything you choose."

"Like something with fur?" snarled the ogre, as he turned into lion!

"Er... what about a little bird?" purred Puss. "Or a mouse?"

Sound out these words with the ur sound.

learn   earth   curl   nurse

girl   third   term   serve

14

Use the stickers to **spell** some more words using the **ur** sound.

early   church   stir   herb

Highlight the ow sound (as in now)

Stick on the speech bubbles for Puss and the ogre.

Sound out these words with the ow sound.

owl   how   town   flower

out   house   ground

16

The ogre growled, and in a flash he became a mouse!

"Now I've got you," shouted Puss loudly, and bounced down from the wall.

He pounced on the mouse, and that was the end of the ogre!

Use your stickers to **finish** the sentence with the **ow** sound.

"Now I've got you," shouted Puss loudly.

The servants in the ogre's castle were very relieved. They thought they would be under the ogre's spell forever.

We will be happy to serve Marquis.

Well done!

Sound out these words, which all have the v sound.

van   vase   wave

seven   velvet

18

To thank Puss, the happy servants organised a perfect party for everyone.

Use your arrow stickers to **point** to two things using the p sound.

Focus on the p sound in different positions

Well done!

Say the words as you spot each thing with the p sound.

Stick on their stickers.

cupcakes

Puss

apples

Highlight the d
sound in different
positions

The next day, the delighted king offered the Marquis of Carabas his daughter's hand in marriage.

Sound out these words with the d sound.

dog   deep   dust   puddle

food   add   played

20

So, Sam the miller's son – now a Marquis – married the princess!

Draw attention to the m sound (as in miller)

Use the stickers to **spell** some words beginning with m.

mug   mat   moth   mess

After that, Puss wasn't even expected to chase mice. He made himself an extra big pot of tea and sat down to relax!

Use your stickers to **spell** some words with the ks blend.

exit   mix   box   wax   six

Ask your child to **retell** the story using
these key sounds and story images.

Sam

Puss

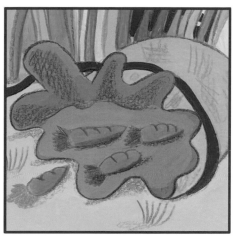
sack

king

drown

ogre

mouse

marry

relax

Use your stickers to **add** a word that matches
the red highlighted **sounds** on each line.

bridge   brush   bramble

thick   thank   thin

clue   room   chew

hop   hit   hen

buzz   these   cheese

big   goose   ogre

girl   term   curl

van   velvet   vase

perfect   apples   happy

24

You've had fun with phonics! Well done.